This edition published by Parragon Books Ltd in 2014

Parragon Books Ltd
Chartist House
15–17 Trim Street
Bath BA1 1HA, UK
www.parragon.com

ISBN 978-1-4723-4693-3

Printed in China

Bath · New York · Singapore · Hong Kong · Cologne · Delhi
Melbourne · Amsterdam · Johannesburg · Shenzhen

One beautiful day in Pixie Hollow, Rosetta, Silvermist and Iridessa were planting sunflowers when Zarina walked past.

"Hey, Zarina! Out of pixie dust again?" asked Rosetta.

Fairies use pixie dust to fly, but Zarina preferred to walk. "Just out for a stroll. You know me!"

Zarina was a dust-keeper fairy and, one day, it was her turn to pour the special Blue Pixie Dust into the Pixie Dust Tree.

The Blue Pixie Dust was powerful – mixing it with golden pixie dust made the gold dust multiply!

Zarina asked Fairy Gary, the head dust-keeper, if they could make other colours of pixie dust. Fairy Gary warned her, "Dust-keepers are forbidden to tamper with pixie dust."

But secretly Zarina had been saving up her pixie dust. After finding a speck of Blue Dust in her hair, Zarina was inspired to try one of her many failed pixie dust experiments again, this time adding a tiny bit of the Blue Dust speck.
The gold dust turned orange!
Zarina shared her discovery with her friend Tinker Bell – the new orange dust allowed Zarina to bend a moonbeam!

Zarina wanted to experiment more! Tink was concerned. "Zarina, I really think you should stop," she said firmly.

Zarina turned and accidentally bumped into a plant, spilling all of her new pink dust on it. The plant's vines grew quickly, bursting out of Zarina's cottage and spreading all over Pixie Hollow. They even crushed the Dust Depot.

Zarina couldn't believe the damage!
When Fairy Gary saw the pink dust, he knew
Zarina had been experimenting with pixie dust.
He told Zarina she could no longer be a
dust-keeper fairy. "You were told not to
tamper with pixie dust."

She was devastated. She rushed
back home, packed her things and
left Pixie Hollow.

One year later, the fairies celebrated the Four Seasons Festival.

While Periwinkle dazzled the crowd at the amphitheatre with her ice-skating skills, Tink and her friends were backstage working on their act for the show.

As everyone watched Periwinkle's performance, Tinker Bell saw a fairy sprinkling pink dust behind the crowd.

"Wait. Is that ... Zarina?" asked Tink.

Suddenly, flowers sprouted in the amphitheatre –
and then they burst open and sprayed
pollen into the air. Rosetta knew
it would make everyone fall
asleep. "Guys! We gotta
hide – now!"

After Tink and her friends came out of hiding, they discovered the Blue Pixie Dust was missing!

They followed its blue glow to a rowing boat where they saw Zarina showing the bag of dust to pirates! Tinker Bell assumed the pirates made Zarina take the dust.

But then the fairies watched in shock as a pirate called James said to Zarina, "Let me say, your plan worked perfectly ... captain."

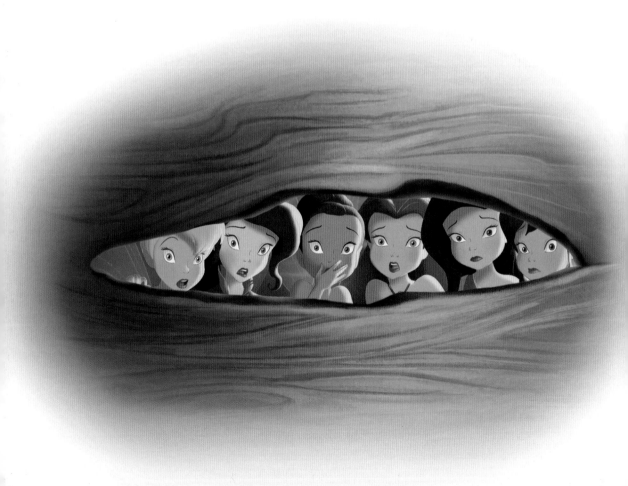

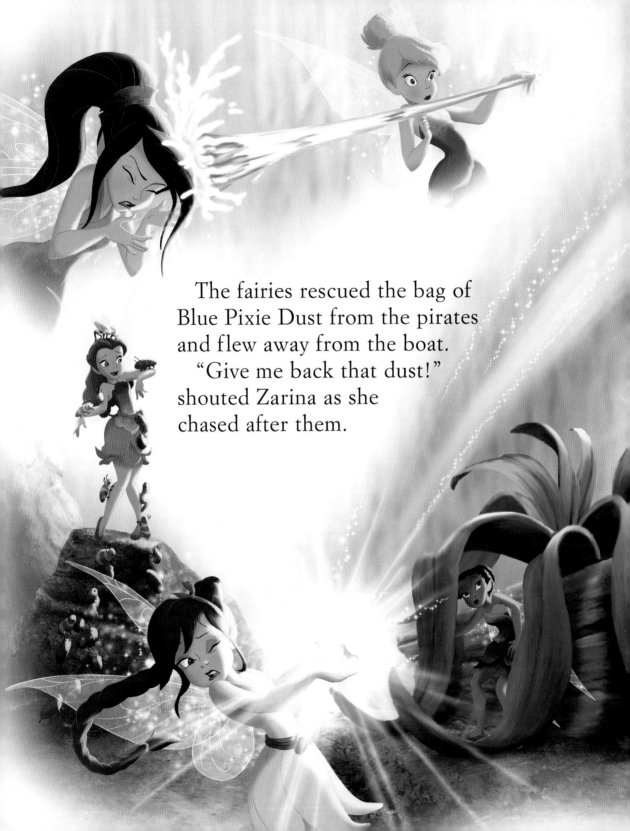

The fairies rescued the bag of
Blue Pixie Dust from the pirates
and flew away from the boat.
"Give me back that dust!"
shouted Zarina as she
chased after them.

She threw multicoloured dust at them, knocking them through the waterfall and out cold. Zarina took back the bag of Blue Pixie Dust and flew off.

When the fairies woke up they discovered that the dust had swapped their talents and their outfits!

With their new talents, the fairies found the pirate ship that the rowing boat had been taking the Blue Pixie Dust to and they sneaked aboard.

The ship sailed to Skull Rock where, inside, Zarina had grown a Pixie Dust Tree. The pirates wanted the pixie dust from the tree to make their ship fly! Some of the fairies sneaked into Zarina's cabin, where they listened to James and Zarina's plans. The others tried to listen from outside.

James watched Zarina preparing the Blue Pixie Dust. "So the secret is to put the Blue Dust directly into the tree. Very impressive, captain!"

Inside Skull Rock, Zarina and James made their way to the tree. Slowly, Zarina tipped the container of Blue Dust into the dust well of the tree. Then she saw the fairies.

Zarina drew her sword and called to her pirate friends, who caught the fairies in nets.

"Zarina, don't do this! Come back home," begged Tinker Bell.

"I'll never go back to Pixie Hollow," answered Zarina. "This is exactly where I belong."

Tink and the others
were taken to the galley,
where the ship's cook put
them in an old crab cage.
The fairies tried their best
to escape, but they were
locked up tight.

Meanwhile, Zarina added
Blue Pixie Dust to the tree,
which then started to make
golden dust flow. The
pirates cheered! Zarina
sprinkled it on James.

She taught him to fly and they soared through the air together. But when they landed back on the ship, James locked Zarina in a lantern. Now that he had the dust, he revealed he had been using her – he had never been her friend.

The fairies finally managed to free themselves and helped Zarina escape from the lantern.

Zarina apologized and offered to help stop the pirates. But the fairies struggled to fight the pirates with their tiny swords.

Suddenly, they realized that if they used their talents together they could defeat the pirates.

Fawn used her new light talent to shoot scorching light-beams down at the pirates. Silvermist, now a fast-flying fairy, created a whirlwind to knock the ship off course.

While Zarina and James fought, the ship started to
tip over. James clung to the mast trying not to fall in
the sea.

Zarina took the vial of Blue Pixie Dust which he
had around his neck. When he saw the golden pixie
dust start to fall from the ship into the
sea he reached for it and fell!

But then James, covered
in golden dust, flew up
behind Zarina. He took the vial
of Blue Pixie Dust back from her,
spilling a speck. "Take it. What's one
speck between friends?" he said.

Zarina threw the speck at him. "No, you
should have it all!"

The speck of Blue Pixie Dust made the gold dust that
was on James multiply and he flew wildly through the air
before plunging into a giant wave!

The fairies congratulated each other on defeating the pirates and turned the ship round.

Zarina gave the vial of Blue Pixie Dust to Tink. "Please take this back to Pixie Hollow," she said.

But Tink was not going to return without her friend.

"Zarina, we didn't come just for the Blue Pixie Dust," said Tink, smiling.

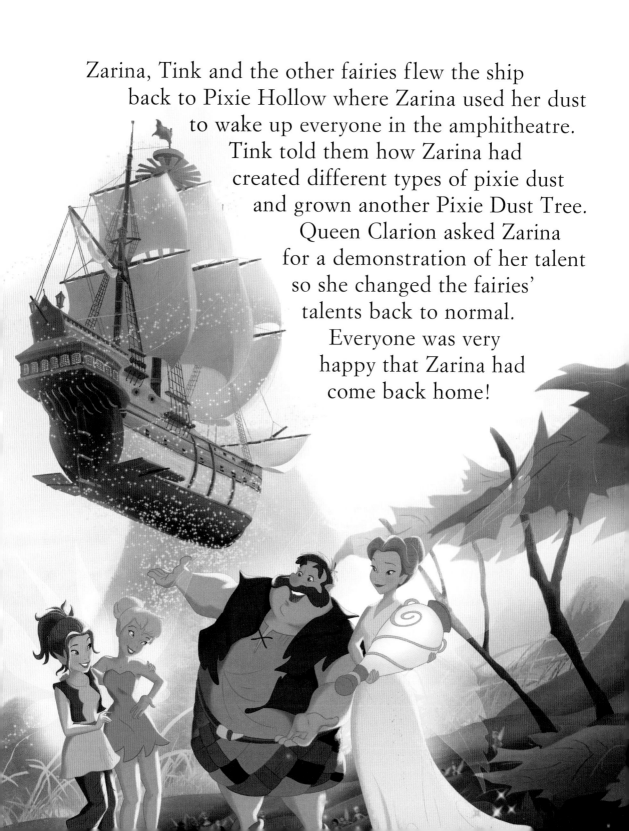

Zarina, Tink and the other fairies flew the ship
back to Pixie Hollow where Zarina used her dust
to wake up everyone in the amphitheatre.
Tink told them how Zarina had
created different types of pixie dust
and grown another Pixie Dust Tree.
Queen Clarion asked Zarina
for a demonstration of her talent
so she changed the fairies'
talents back to normal.
Everyone was very
happy that Zarina had
come back home!